39 Kids on the Block™

The Best Present Ever

by Jean Marzollo

illustrated by Irene Trivas

SCHOLASTIC INC.

New York   Toronto   London   Auckland   Sydney

Look for these and other books
in the **39 Kids on the Block** series:

#1 *The Green Ghost of Appleville*
#2 *The Best Present Ever*
#3 *Roses Are Pink and You Stink!*
#4 *Best Friends*

ISBN 0-590-42724-5

Copyright © 1989 by Jean Marzollo.
All rights reserved. Published by Scholastic Inc.
39 KIDS ON THE BLOCK is a trademark of Scholastic Inc.

12 11 10 9 8 7 6 5 4 3 2   9/8 0 1 2 3 4/9

Printed in the U.S.A.   11

First Scholastic printing, December 1989

For Greg, Roger, Luke, Travis,
Vanessa, Patrizia, Jessica, Vinny,
Kyle, Christian, Justin, Anthony,
Alison, Michael, Toni, Tanya,
Jillian, Corinne, and Mrs. Petroccione
—J.M.

For the children of Nancy Leete's class
at Woodsville Elementary School,
Woodsville, N.H. *—I.T.*

Thirty-nine kids live on Baldwin Street.
They range in age from babies to teenagers.
The main kids in this story are:
Rusty Morelli
Mary Kate Adams
Jane Fox
Fizz Eddie Fox
Kimberly Brown
Michael Finn
John Beane
Maria Lopez
Lisa Wu

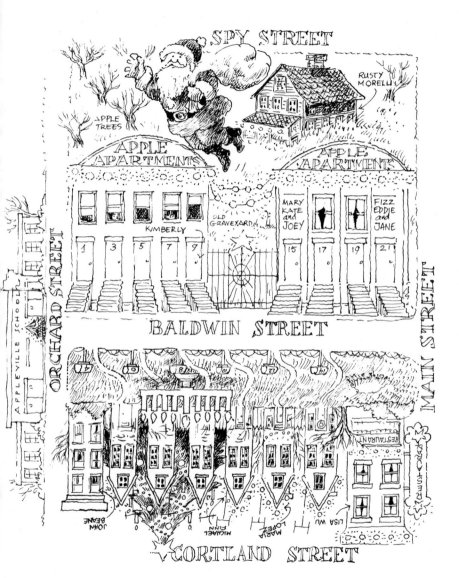

Chapter 1

Rusty Morelli was lying on the bear rug in the living room. Mighty Mouse was on TV.

It was a rainy Saturday morning in December.

"I like Mighty Mouse," said Mrs. Morelli. Mrs. Morelli was Rusty's grandmother. She was also an artist.

Mrs. Morelli was painting a big picture in the living room. Her overalls had paint on them. So did her nose and cheeks.

One end of the painting stuck into the

dining room. The other end stuck into the hall.

Rusty didn't understand the painting. It looked like dancing triangles to him.

"Wham-bang!" said the TV. A remote-control race car went up a hill. A boy on TV was playing with it. It was a Christmas present.

"What do *you* want for Christmas?" asked Mrs. Morelli.

"I don't care," said Rusty.

"You don't care? Why not? Christmas is coming!" said his grandma.

Christmas without my parents, thought Rusty. But he didn't say that because he didn't want his grandma to feel bad.

She was taking care of him for a year. His parents were in Brazil. They were studying trees in the jungle.

"All this rain makes me miss California," said Mrs. Morelli.

"Me, too," said Rusty.

Rusty and his parents used to live in

California. It was sunny there.

His grandmother had lived there, too. Then she moved to an old house in Appleville, New Jersey. Her grandfather used to live there.

Rusty had a choice. He could either go to Brazil or to Appleville.

He wanted to go with his parents. But there was no school in the jungle. And there were no kids to play with.

Rusty's grandma said Rusty could help her move. She said she needed him.

So Rusty chose Appleville. And he liked it, too. But he sure did miss his mom and dad.

In a year his parents would be back. Then they would live with him and his grandma. A big room waited for them upstairs.

Mrs. Morelli dropped her brush in a coffee can. "Enough is enough," she said. "Tell you what. Turn off the boob tube. Let's make pancakes."

In the kitchen Rusty measured the milk. His grandmother added the pancake mix. Rusty stirred the batter, but not too much. It was supposed to be lumpy.

"What kind of pancakes do you want today?" said his grandmother. "Teddy bears?"

"I don't care," said Rusty.

"Stop saying that!" said his grandmother. "It's very important to care. Now, guess what this is."

His grandma dropped a big circle of batter on the griddle. Then another medium circle touching the big one. And then a small one for the head.

"A snowman!" said Rusty.

"Right," said his grandmother. "Maybe you'll get to make a real one this winter."

Mrs. Morelli made another snowman on the griddle.

"I have an idea," said Rusty. He took the cup and started to pour. "Guess what this is."

Rusty made an X with batter on the griddle. Then he put a line across the X.

"A snowflake!" said his grandma. "Make some more. Make a blizzard!"

Rusty made four more snowflakes. Then he and his grandmother ate the snowmen and the snowflakes with butter and blueberry syrup.

Afterwards they let Blackie the cat lick the plates. Blackie was a white cat. Mrs. Morelli had named him Blackie as a joke.

Rusty sat on his grandma's lap. "Do you think my mom and dad will call today?" he asked.

Rusty's parents tried to call every Saturday. But sometimes the phone in the jungle didn't work.

Thinking about his parents made Rusty start to cry.

"I know how you feel," said his grandma. "But if they do call, try not to act too sad. They're sad, too. They would love to come home for Christmas. But it costs too much money."

Rusty's grandmother gave him a big hug. She smelled like soap and paint. He loved her very much, but . . . she wasn't his mom and dad.

"What should I tell them?" asked Rusty.

"Tell them what we're going to do for Christmas."

"What *are* we going to do?" asked Rusty.

"I don't know," said his grandmother. "To tell you the truth, I'm not crazy about Christmas. But we'll think of something."

Mrs. Morelli got up to wash the dishes. Rusty cleared the table.

"Are we going to get a tree?" he asked.

"We can't put it in the living room," said his grandma. "My painting's too big. But we could put it in the kitchen."

"That would be weird," said Rusty. "Are we going to make Christmas cookies with frosting and sprinkles?"

"Too sweet," said his grandmother. "Maybe on Christmas morning we'll make Christmas tree pancakes."

"Can we go shopping at the mall?" asked Rusty.

"I hate malls," said his grandmother. "And besides, I have no money to spend. This year let's *make* our presents. You make me a painting. And I'll make you one."

Rusty felt like crying again.

He didn't want a painting. He wanted a Christmas tree in the living room. He wanted his mom home baking cookies. And his dad taking him to the mall.

He wanted a normal Christmas with a normal family.

"Are we going to go to church?" he asked.

His grandmother stopped washing dishes. "It's possible," she said.

Rusty guessed she meant no.

Rusty always went to church on Christmas Eve with his mom and dad. His grandmother usually stayed home. She said her church was in her paintings.

"Cheer up," said his grandmother. "We

had a good Halloween, didn't we? Remember the haunted house?"

But Rusty couldn't cheer up.

Suddenly the telephone rang.

Rusty picked it up and said hello.

"Rusty!" said his mom. "How are you?"

"Guess what?" said his dad. "We have a surprise!"

"What is it?" asked Rusty.

"We saved two thousand dollars," said his mom. "So we're coming home for Christmas!"

"That's great!" cried Rusty. "Grandma, they're coming home!"

Mrs. Morelli threw her dish towel in the air. "Yippee!" she said.

That night Rusty listened to Blackie purring on his bed. Rusty was so happy, he wished he could purr, too.

It rained all day Sunday. But Rusty and his grandmother didn't mind.

Rusty started a painting of California

for his dad. He wondered what his parents would bring him as a present from Brazil. He couldn't wait to see.

Once his parents had studied trees in Japan. When they came home, they brought Rusty a real samurai sword.

The sword turned out to be very old. And valuable. A man at the museum said it was worth a lot of money.

The sword hung over his grandmother's fireplace. It was in a black leather case. Rusty looked at it and felt proud.

He also looked at his grandmother's painting. "Is that a picture of dancing triangles?" he asked.

"Yes," said his grandmother. "Do you like it?"

"Sure," said Rusty.

"Then it's yours," said his grandma. "For Christmas." She smiled at him proudly.

Rusty grinned. He didn't mind getting a painting now that his parents were coming home. "Where will I put it?" he asked. "It's too big for my room."

"Put it anywhere you want," said his grandma.

Rusty had no idea where he'd put the huge painting. But it didn't matter. He was too excited to worry.

Chapter 2

Monday morning it was still raining. Rusty walked to school with his friends.

Mary Kate and Jane shared a Snoopy umbrella.

Fizz Eddie, Jane's older brother, wore his football jacket. He didn't seem to care if his head got wet.

Fizz Eddie was in junior high. He got his nickname from being good at phys. ed.

His friend, Kimberly, was also in junior

high. She had a pink umbrella. Fizz Eddie wouldn't get under it. He walked next to Rusty.

Rusty wore a Dodgers jacket and a Dodgers cap. The Dodgers were from California. Just like Rusty and his grandmother.

"Hey, Champ!" said Fizz Eddie. He called Rusty "Champ" because the Dodgers won the World Series in 1988. "How do you like the snow?"

Rusty looked up. Big drops of water fell on his face. "I thought snow was white and fluffy," he said.

Everyone laughed.

"Fizz Eddie is joking," said Mary Kate. "Snow *is* white and fluffy."

"Each flake is a tiny star," said Jane. "And each one is different. Millions of different snowflakes fall all at once."

"Wow," said Rusty. He tried to imagine snow, but he couldn't.

Fizz Eddie began to sing. "I'm dreaming of a white Hanukkah."

Everyone laughed again, even Rusty. This time he got the joke. Fizz Eddie said "Hanukkah" because he was Jewish. The real song said, "I'm dreaming of a white Christmas."

Rusty felt good.

It was fun to walk to school with his new friends in Appleville. Even in the rain.

It was fun to think about Christmas, too. And snow. And most of all, his parents. He couldn't wait to see them!

Every day Rusty's teacher, Mr. Carson, wore clip-on bow ties. Today his tie was red and green. "For the holidays," he said.

"Are we going to have a Christmas party?" asked Rusty. Maybe his mom and dad could come.

"Or a Hanukkah party?" asked Jane.

"Let's have both," said Mr. Carson. "And if there are other holidays, we'll have a party for them, too."

Michael Finn's hand shot into the air. "Want me to make a party chart?" he asked.

Michael liked to make charts and maps.

On the wall was a map he had made of his block. It showed where the kids on the block lived. Rusty was one of them.

There were 39 kids in all, so the title of the map was "39 Kids on the Block."

Michael also had made a "39 Kids" map for Halloween. And he was going to make another one for Valentine's Day.

Mr. Carson liked the maps. He liked anything with numbers. Math was Mr. Carson's favorite subject.

Now he said to Michael, "A party chart would be very helpful. I'll tell you what, Michael. You can wear my bow tie and be the teacher."

Mr. Carson put his bow tie on Michael Finn. Then Mr. Carson sat in Michael's seat.

Michael Finn went to the front of the class. He drew a big chart on the board.

Rusty looked at the wall above the chalkboard. It had a big crack in it. Every time the school fixed it, the crack came back.

The principal said the crack wasn't dangerous. But Mr. Carson hated it. He liked his classroom to be nice and neat.

Maybe Michael should make a really big map to hang over the crack, thought Rusty.

Michael wrote: NAME, PARTY, and WHAT TO DO on the chart.

"How about also writing what people want for a present?" said Mary Kate. "I want a puppy more than anything."

"But nobody is going to give you a puppy at the school party," said Michael.

"So what?" said Jane.

"Raise your hand if you want to put presents on the chart. Even if your present has nothing to do with the school party," said Michael Finn.

Hands flew into the air.

So Michael Finn wrote PRESENT on the chart, too.

"Who wants to go first?" he asked.

Mary Kate raised her hand.

Michael Finn wrote *M.K.A.* for Mary Kate Adams under NAME. He also wrote *puppy* under PRESENT. "Your party?" he asked.

"I want to have a Christmas party at school," said Mary Kate. "We can bake cookies and decorate a tree. For my present I want a puppy."

"You already said that," said Michael Finn. "Next?"

Jane Fox raised her hand. "I would like to have a Hanukkah party. We can light candles and spin a dreidel. For a present I want a rabbit-fur muff."

"Very good," said Michael Finn. He was amazing. He could spell everything, even dreidel. "Next?"

Rusty raised his hand. "I want to have a Christmas party, too," he said. "And I agree with Mary Kate about what to do."

"What do you want for a present?" asked Michael.

This was the moment Rusty had been

waiting for. "I want my parents to bring me a surprise," he said.

"Your parents?" asked Michael. "I thought they were in Brazil."

"They're coming home for Christmas," said Rusty with a big grin. Everyone could see his halfway-grown front teeth.

Michael Finn wrote *surprise* on the board.

"I also want snow," said Rusty. "I've never seen it before."

"Is it okay to have two things?" asked Michael.

"Yes," said Mr. Carson. "If the second thing doesn't cost money."

Michael Finn wrote *snow* next to *surprise*.

"Next?" he asked.

John Beane raised his hand. "We have an American Indian Christmas," he said. "My mother is Creek. She hangs native beadwork on our tree. My father is Sioux. He puts my eagle feathers on the tallest branch."

"Eagle feathers?" asked Rusty.

"The eagle flies highest of all the birds," said John. "The feathers were given to me when I was a baby. I was very small when I was born. The feathers helped me to grow strong."

"Maybe we could make paper feathers for our class tree," said Mary Kate.

"To make us strong," said Rusty.

Michael wrote *feathers* on the chart.

"Your present?" he asked.

"A remote control racing car," said John.

"Can I go next?" asked Michael. "Even though I'm the teacher?"

"Sure," said Mr. Carson.

Under HOLIDAY Michael Finn wrote *Kwanzaa.*

"What's that?" asked John.

"Kwanzaa is a new holiday," said Michael Finn. "It lasts seven days. It's African-American. I'm learning about it at church."

"What do you do on Kwanzaa?" asked Jane.

"You make presents to give to people you love," said Michael.

My grandmother would like Kwanzaa, thought Rusty.

Under WHAT TO DO Michael wrote *make presents*. Under PRESENT he wrote *army men*.

Then he looked sad and added *teeth*.

Everyone knew why. Michael still had all his baby teeth. He was the only one. And they weren't even loose.

Maria Lopez raised her hand. "I want to have a Three Kings Day party. That's a special party on January 6th. We can make *piñatas*. For my present I want a doll."

Lisa Wu raised her hand. "I want a Christmas party with Chinese food," she said. "For my present I want a pair of ice skates."

Michael Finn wrote down their holidays. The chart now looked like this:

NAME	HOLIDAY	WHAT TO DO	PRESENT
M.K.	Christmas	Cookies, tree	Puppy
J.F.	Hanukkah	Candles, dreidel	Muff
R.M.	Christmas	Cookies, tree	Surprise Snow
J.B.	Christmas	Feathers	Racing car
M.F.	Kwanzaa	Make presents	Army men
M.L.	Three Kings	Piñatas	Doll
L.W.	Christmas	Chinese food	Ice skates

"We have a problem," said Jane. "Too many holidays."

Mr. Carson stood up. "I agree. And I'm glad. Because I like problems. Know why?"

The kids smiled.

"Because they're mathematical," said Mary Kate.

But Rusty didn't understand. "How is the party problem mathematical?" he asked.

"Every problem has a solution," said Mr. Carson. He took his bow tie back and put it on. "First we can brainstorm a list of solutions. And then we can vote on the best one."

"Yippee, brainstorming!" said Michael Finn. Michael Finn loved brainstorming.

Brainstorming was listing ideas. Michael *always* had ideas. "Here's my first idea," he said. "We can write down all the parties. Then we put the names in a box and draw one."

Mr. Carson started a new chart on the board. At the top he wrote PROBLEM: TOO MANY PARTIES.

Under that he wrote SOLUTIONS. Under that he wrote Michael's idea.

"Ooh-ooh-ooh," said Michael, waving

his hand in the air. "I have more ideas."

"Let's give the others a chance," said Mr. Carson.

"Have all the parties at the same time in the gym," said Maria.

"Have a combination party in our room," said Mary Kate. "We can have food and games for each holiday."

"Let's invent a brand-new holiday," said John. "One that everyone celebrates the same way."

Lisa raised her hand. "I have an idea I don't like," she said. "But I think you should list it. Have no parties at all."

"Yes, and I have another idea," said Mr. Carson. "We can have a party to celebrate the darkest day of the year."

The last idea on the list was Rusty's. "Have a silly party," he said. "We can wear silly clothes and spill food on them."

Everyone liked Rusty's idea except for Mr. Carson. He wrote it down anyway.

"Seven possible solutions," said Mr.

Carson. Everyone looked at the chart. It read:

SOLUTIONS

1. Pick one party out of a hat.
2. Have all parties at the same time in the gym.
3. Have a combination party.
4. Invent a new holiday for everyone.
5. Have no parties at all.
6. Have a darkest-day-of-the-year party.
7. Have a silly party.

"I have another idea," said Rusty. "Whatever party we have, let's invite parents."

"Good idea," said Mr. Carson. "But we don't need to vote on it. So I won't write it down."

"Can I make a ballot box?" asked Michael. "Like a Valentine box? Everyone will write down their vote and put it in the slot."

"Fine," said Mr. Carson.

Rusty raised his hand. "If you want, we can make it at my house," he said. "My grandmother has lots of paint."

"Good idea," said Michael.

Maria raised her hand. "What do *you* want for a present, Mr. Carson?" she asked.

Mr. Carson smiled. "I want Santa Claus to cover up that ugly crack over the chalkboard," he said.

Chapter 3

Rusty and Michael ran into Rusty's house. They were dripping wet.

"Grandma!" shouted Rusty. "Michael Finn came home with me. We're going to make a ballot box! We're going to vote for holiday parties!"

Suddenly Rusty stopped. Something was very wrong.

Water dripped into bowls on the floor. His grandmother was painting under an umbrella. Plastic trash bags covered the ends of her painting.

"What happened?" he asked.

"The roof is leaking," said his grandma.

Rusty took Michael into the kitchen. There, water was dripping into four more bowls.

"At least the table is dry," said Mrs. Morelli. "You can work on your ballot box there."

"How much does it cost to fix a roof?" asked Michael Finn.

"Not too much, I hope," said Mrs. Morelli. "Someone's coming later to look at it and tell me."

Mrs. Morelli found a dry box and cut a slot in the lid. "Here," she said. "Use this. You can use my paint and brushes, too."

Michael Finn asked Mrs. Morelli about her painting. "Is it a picture of a space galaxy?" he said.

"Yes," said Mrs. Morelli.

"But you told me it was dancing triangles," said Rusty.

"It's that, too," his grandmother said.

Rusty showed Michael his painting of California. People were swimming under a big yellow sun.

"Is that what California really looks like?" asked Michael.

"Yes," said Rusty. "Last year we went swimming on Christmas."

"Let's paint a big sun on the ballot box," said Michael.

"I was thinking of a big snowflake," said Rusty.

The two boys looked at each other. They didn't want to fight.

"What do you think, Mrs. Morelli?" asked Michael.

"Both," she said.

"That doesn't make sense," said Michael.

"It will if it's beautiful," she said.

And that's how Rusty and Michael painted a most unusual ballot box. It was blue with yellow suns and white snowflakes.

Just as Rusty was adding the last sun,

the doorbell rang. It was the roofer, Mr. O'Brien.

Mr. O'Brien walked with Mrs. Morelli through the whole house. Rusty and Michael followed them.

There were leaks everywhere. Water was even dripping into a bowl on Rusty's bed.

Then Mr. O'Brien climbed out on the roof. He looked around carefully. Afterwards he sat in the kitchen and had a cup of coffee.

"You need a new roof," he said.

"How much does that cost?" asked Mrs. Morelli.

"Two thousand dollars," said Mr. O'Brien.

"I don't have two thousand dollars," said Mrs. Morelli. "I have paintings. You want to buy a painting for two thousand dollars?"

Mr. O'Brien shook his head. "I don't have two thousand dollars, either," he said.

On his way out, Mr. O'Brien looked at Mrs. Morelli's painting. "Is that a picture of a circus?" he asked.

"Yes," said Mrs. Morelli.

Rusty and Michael looked at Mrs. Morelli in surprise. She winked at them.

"Well, I sure hope someone needs a painting of a circus," said Mr. O'Brien. "Because you have to get your roof fixed right away. Otherwise your house will be ruined."

Mr. O'Brien left, and Michael went home.

Mrs. Morelli and Rusty tried to paint. They held umbrellas in one hand and paint brushes in the other.

"It's no good," said Mrs. Morelli. "All I hear is water dripping. Let's have supper."

Rusty and his grandmother had tofu burgers for supper. As they ate, Rusty talked about the vote at school.

Mrs. Morelli didn't say much. Rusty didn't understand why. Usually she liked to talk.

That night Rusty had to move his bed away from a drip. But in the middle of the night, he felt a drop on his neck.

"Hey!" he cried.

Blackie leaped off the bed. "Meow!" he said.

Rusty moved to a dry part of the bed. Then he tried to go back to sleep. But not with Blackie. He slept under the bed.

The next morning Mrs. Morelli made teddy bear pancakes.

"I got through to your parents last night," she said. "I told them about the roof."

"Did you tell them you were going to sell your big painting to pay for it?" asked Rusty.

"I gave that painting to you," said his grandma. "It's your Christmas present."

"I know," said Rusty. "But if you need the money, you can have it back and sell it."

His grandmother shook her head sadly. "I was only kidding when I said Mr. O'Brien could buy my painting," she said. "I never sell my paintings. I'm afraid people won't like them."

Rusty was surprised. He didn't think his grandmother was afraid of anything.

She went on. "Mr. O'Brien has to fix the roof when the rain stops. And we have to pay him. Your parents are going to send me the money."

"Then why are you so sad?" asked Rusty. He still didn't understand.

"I'm sad because of the two thousand dollars your mom and dad are sending," she said. "That was the money they had saved for Christmas."

"You mean . . .?" Rusty couldn't say the words.

"They can't come home for Christmas," said his grandmother.

Mrs. Morelli put her head down on the

table. Blackie jumped up and touched his nose to her cheek.

Rusty had never seen his grandmother cry before. He felt terrible. Terrible about his parents and terrible about his grand- mother.

Mrs. Morelli reached out an arm. She put it around Rusty and pulled him close. Rusty lay his head on her sweatshirt. Then he cried, too.

After a few minutes, Mrs. Morelli sat up. She pulled two handkerchiefs out of her overalls. She gave the Mickey Mouse one to Rusty. She used the Minnie Mouse one herself.

"I'm sorry, Rusty," she said. "I wish I had more money. Believe me. If I could sell my paintings, I would buy you the moon."

Rusty nodded and tried to smile.

"That's the spirit," she said. "Now hurry up, or you'll be late to school. The skies are still gray. Put the ballot box in a plastic bag just in case the rain starts again."

"I hate the ballot box now," said Rusty.

"Me, too," said his grandmother. "But you have to admit — it's very beautiful."

Chapter 4

"Hey, champ!" said Fizz Eddie. "What's in the trash bag?"

"A stupid ballot box," said Rusty.

"We're voting on our school party today," said Jane.

"Christmas is stupid," said Rusty.

"What's so stupid about it?" asked Fizz Eddie.

"My parents can't come home," said Rusty. "The money they saved has to go for a new roof."

"That's tough," said Fizz Eddie. "I'm sorry to hear about it."

"I wanted my parents to come to the school party," said Rusty. "Now I don't want a party at all."

"Me, neither," said Mary Kate. "I hate Christmas, and I hate my mother, too. She won't let me get a puppy."

"Why not?" asked Fizz Eddie.

"She says I'm not old enough to take care of it," said Mary Kate. "She says she has her hands full with me and Joey."

"I don't want a party, either," said Jane. "I hate Hanukkah. My father says I can't have a rabbit-fur muff. He says it's wrong to kill animals for their fur."

Fizz Eddie shook his head. "What a gloomy bunch of kids you are," he said. "I want an electronic keyboard for Hanukkah. And my wish is going to come true."

"How do you know?" asked Jane, his sister.

"Because I already picked it out," said Fizz Eddie. "And Mom already paid for it."

"You always get more than me," said Jane.

Fizz Eddie ignored her. He waved to Kimberly Brown. She was waiting for him on her stoop.

Kimberly had a ponytail and snowflake earrings. She was in junior high school, too.

"Hi, Fizz," she said. She didn't say hi to the younger kids. "What are you and your sister fighting about?"

"Tell me," said Fizz Eddie. "Do you like the holidays? Christmas, Hanukkah, presents, candy, and all that stuff?"

"I love them!" she said.

"Me, too," he said. "But these kids belong to the Gloom and Doom Gang. They hate the holidays."

"Ooh, the poor little things," said Kimberly.

"'Ooh, the poor little things,'" said Jane, copying her. Luckily, Kimberly didn't hear. She and Fizz Eddie were walking behind.

"Nice ballot box," said Mr. Carson.

Rusty said nothing. He wrote *no party* on a piece of paper. Then he dropped his ballot in the slot. So did the rest of the Gloom and Doom Gang.

Soon everyone had voted.

Michael Finn opened the box and counted the votes. "There are eighteen votes in all," he said. "Three for PICK ONE PARTY OUT OF A HAT. Two for HAVE ALL PARTIES AT THE SAME TIME. Four for HAVE A COMBINATION PARTY. Two for INVENT A NEW HOLIDAY FOR EVERYONE. Four for HAVE A SILLY PARTY. And three for HAVE NO PARTIES AT ALL."

Maria was shocked. "Who doesn't want to have a party?" she asked.

"It was a secret ballot," said Mr. Carson. "So we'll never know."

Rusty was glad he didn't have to raise his hand.

"It's a tie between the combination party and the silly party," said John.

"I'm afraid so," said Mr. Carson. "Now we'll have to vote again on all the parties. But let me say this about the Silly Party. You can wear silly clothes. But there will be no spilling food on them. Is that clear?"

Michael Finn passed out paper. Everyone began to vote again.

Rusty didn't know how to vote. He looked over at Jane. She wasn't writing.

He looked over at Mary Kate. She wasn't writing, either.

Rusty wondered if they were still in the gloom and doom gang.

He wondered if the class *should* have a party, even if his parents couldn't come. Just because he wouldn't have fun didn't mean the others shouldn't.

Mary Kate raised her hand. "If we have a combination party, can we have a Christmas tree?" she asked.

"And spin the dreidel?" asked Jane.

"Yes," said Mr. Carson.

Mary Kate and Jane began to write. Rusty knew they were voting for the Combination Party. So he wrote Silly Party on his ballot.

This time Maria counted the ballots. "The results are: Three votes for PICK ONE PARTY OUT OF A HAT. Two for HAVE ALL PARTIES AT THE SAME TIME. Six for HAVE A COMBINATION PARTY. Two for INVENT A NEW HOLIDAY FOR EVERYONE. And five for HAVE A SILLY PARTY. The combination party wins."

Kids cheered. Mr. Carson looked pleased.

"We can call it 'Happy, Happy Holidays,' " said Jane.

"Good idea," said Mr. Carson.

"And we can sing different songs," said Maria. "I know a special song for Three Kings Day."

"I know a good song, too," said Jane, clapping her hands. " 'Dreidel, dreidel, dreidel,' " she sang.

" 'Oh, Christmas tree, oh, Christmas tree,' " sang Michael Finn. Other kids started singing songs, too.

Mr. Carson pretended he was conducting the class. But it sounded awful because everyone was singing a different song.

Finally Mr. Carson opened his top desk drawer. He took out a little bell and rang it. The singing stopped.

"I think we're going to have a great party," he said. "And you know what I like best about it?"

"It's mathematical," said John.

"That's right," said Mr. Carson. "We have to vote on the food and games we want. We have to collect money. We have to buy paper plates and napkins. We have to follow recipes. And we have to count the number of people we want to invite."

"Don't count my parents," said Rusty. "They'll be in Brazil."

Chapter 5

Rusty was making a paper chain for the Happy, Happy Holidays tree. But he was not happy, happy.

Other kids were making food for the party. John and Michael were decorating the tree.

Some kids' parents were helping out. But not Rusty's parents. They were five thousand miles away.

Rusty tried not to think of them. He hung his chain on the class tree. It looked stupid.

Michael and John thought the tree looked great. Everyone was cheerful except Rusty.

When he went home, he found his grandmother painting. She seemed cheerful, too.

Mr. O'Brien was working on the roof. As he worked, he played rock and roll on a boom box. Usually rock and roll bothered Mrs. Morelli.

Rusty watched his grandmother paint another red triangle.

"Grandma," said Rusty. "How come the music doesn't bother you? How come you're so happy?"

Mrs. Morelli sighed. "I'm not really happy," she said. "I wanted your mom and dad to come home. But I got a new roof instead. That's life. You can't always get what you want."

And you can't always want what you get, thought Rusty. He looked at the big painting. It wasn't what he wanted at all. It wasn't even close.

*   *   *

That night when Rusty went to bed, he told his troubles to Blackie. He was lying on Rusty's stomach and purring.

"I have a problem," he said. "I want my parents to come home for Christmas."

Blackie listened. He was a good student. He made Rusty feel like a teacher.

"Every problem has a solution," said Rusty. He sounded just like Mr. Carson. "And I like problems. They're mathematical."

Blackie stood up and stretched.

"What's that?" said Rusty. "You want to brainstorm solutions? Okay. Here goes: One. We could *not* get a new roof." But Rusty knew that solution wouldn't work.

"Two. We could sell my grandmother's paintings." His grandmother had many paintings. They were hanging all over the house. But she was afraid to sell them. So that wouldn't work either.

"Three. We could sell something else. But what?"

Suddenly Rusty had an idea. He leaped

out of bed and ran downstairs. Blackie ran after him.

His grandmother was lying on the bear rug. She was watching a movie on TV. "Bad dream?" she asked.

Rusty looked up at his samurai sword.

"You dreamed of your sword?" asked his grandmother.

"Sort of," said Rusty. "But it's okay. 'Night."

He gave his grandmother a kiss. Then he picked up Blackie and went to bed.

On Monday Rusty asked Fizz Eddie to take him to the museum.

"I have basketball practice after school," said Fizz Eddie. "But I could take you Saturday morning."

"Okay," said Rusty.

That night he told his grandmother he was going to the museum with Fizz Eddie on Saturday. "Isn't that nice," she said.

She didn't know what he was planning to do.

Rusty didn't tell her because he didn't know if she would agree to his plan.

On Tuesday he felt much happier at school. He helped Jane make a blue-and-white Hanukkah banner.

He helped John string beads for the tree.

He helped Lisa Wu and her mother make Chinese egg rolls.

"If my mother were here, she'd come to school, too," he said.

Jane and Maria came over to help. "Is there a Santa Claus or not?" Maria asked Mrs. Wu.

"What do you think?" asked Mrs. Wu.

"I think there is," said Maria.

"I think you're right," said Mrs. Wu.

"Hanukkah started three days ago," said Jane. "I already got three presents."

"What did you get?" asked Maria.

"A baby doll, a teenage doll, and a lady doll," said Jane.

"No muff yet?" asked Maria.

"No, but I'm still hoping," said Jane.

"I really hope you get one," said Maria.

"Me, too," said Rusty.

On Wednesday Mrs. Peterson, the music teacher, came to class. She helped the children practice their medley.

"Let's take it from the top," she said.

The children sang "The Mexican Hat Dance" and "Dreidel, Dreidel, Dreidel."

Usually "The Mexican Hat Dance" didn't have words. But Mrs. Peterson had made some up for the song. Then they sang "Jingle Bells" and "Kumbaya."

"Not bad," said Mrs. Peterson. "Not bad at all."

Mr. Finn came to school in the afternoon. He helped the kids make Kwanzaa presents for their parents.

Some kids made pencil holders from

juice cans. Some made napkin holders from cereal boxes. And some made tissue carnations.

On Thursday Fizz Eddie and Kimberly visited the class.

"The junior high is making a Giving Tree," said Kimberly. "We're collecting presents for children and hanging them on the tree. On the last day of school we'll give the presents to poor people."

"So please bring in a wrapped toy on Friday," said Fizz Eddie. "If you do, you can come in the blue door. We'll help you hang your present on the tree."

The blue door at the Appleville School was only for junior high kids. Kids in elementary school used the green door.

As Fizz Eddie left, he said to Rusty, "See you Saturday, Champ."

Everyone was jealous. They wanted to know what Rusty and Fizz Eddie were going to do.

"It's a secret," said Rusty.

Rusty was getting more and more excited about Christmas.

"My parents *can* come to the school party," he announced. "They're coming home from Brazil."

"I thought they didn't have the money," said Mary Kate.

"They're getting it," said Rusty.

But he didn't say how — yet.

"I don't want *my* parents to come," said Mary Kate.

"Why not?" asked Rusty.

"My mother still won't let me get a puppy," said Mary Kate. "So you know what I did? My dad asked me to help him pick out a quilt for her as a present. I picked out the ugliest one there was. I hope she hates it."

Rusty was shocked. "What's it like?" he asked.

"It has orange flowers and purple leaves,"

said Mary Kate. "It's really gross."

On Friday Rusty brought a wrapped puzzle to school. Mary Kate brought a wrapped ball. Jane brought a wrapped doll.

They walked in the blue door with Fizz Eddie and Kimberly.

There they saw a big tree that the junior high school kids had made. It reached to the top of the ceiling. It had wooden branches with hooks on them.

Fizz Eddie lifted Rusty up. Rusty hung his present high on the tree.

John Beane came in the blue door with his grandfather. John hung his present on the tree, too.

John's grandfather put a real eagle feather on top of the Giving Tree. Then he said a blessing for the poor people who would get the food. "The eagle flies highest of all the birds," he said.

Rusty shivered. He felt as strong as an eagle. He imagined he was an eagle. He flew all the way to Brazil. He imagined his

parents were eagles, too. They flew back with him to New Jersey.

"See you tomorrow morning, Champ," said Fizz Eddie. "I'll pick you up at ten."

"I'll be waiting," said Rusty.

Chapter 6

Saturday morning Rusty got up early and dressed quickly.

On the way downstairs, he peeked into his grandmother's room. She was still sleeping.

Good.

Rusty crept downstairs. He stood on a chair in front of the fireplace. He took down his samurai sword. It was heavy.

Rusty wrapped the sword in newspaper. Then he put it in his school backpack. He stuffed more paper around it.

Rusty ate some cereal. He sat on the bear rug and watched cartoons. After a while, his grandmother came downstairs. She got a cup of coffee and watched cartoons with him.

Then she started painting.

She never noticed that the sword was missing.

At ten o'clock Fizz Eddie came by. "Hi, Mrs. Morelli," he said. He looked at her painting. "Is that a painting of a football game?" he asked.

"Yes," said Mrs. Morelli.

Rusty laughed. He put on his jacket and his backpack. "'Bye, Grandma," he said. "See you later."

"Have a good time at the museum," she said.

Rusty and Fizz Eddie went to a special office at the back of the museum. Rusty remembered where it was. He had gone there before with his dad.

A man was working at his desk. He was studying a painting.

"Excuse me," said Rusty. "I'd like to sell my samurai sword."

The man came over. Fizz Eddie took the sword out of Rusty's backpack.

The man took it out of its case. "It's a beauty," he said.

"You told my father it was worth two thousand dollars," said Rusty.

"I remember," said the man.

"My parents are in Brazil," said Rusty. "They saved two thousand dollars to come home for Christmas. But my grandmother needed the money to buy a new roof. So now they can't come home. If I sell the sword, I'll have two thousand dollars. And then my parents can come home!"

The man raised his eyebrows. "How long will they be home?" he asked.

"About a week," said Rusty.

"Then they'll go back to Brazil," said the man. "And you won't have the sword anymore."

"I know," said Rusty.

"The value of this sword will grow," said the man. "In two years it may be worth four thousand dollars."

"Hey, Champ," said Fizz Eddie. "You see what the man's saying? He's saying maybe you shouldn't sell the sword."

The man nodded. "Do your parents know you're here?" he asked.

"No," said Rusty. As he said it, he felt a lump in his throat.

The man took a deep breath. "Does your grandmother know you're here?"

"She knows we're at the museum," said Rusty.

"But she doesn't know you have the sword," said the man.

Rusty felt his lower lip quiver. He bit the inside with his teeth so he wouldn't cry. He could tell his plan wasn't going to work.

Fizz Eddie put his arm around Rusty and gave him a squeeze.

"I'm sorry," said the man. "But I can't help you. I can't buy the sword without permission from your parents."

Suddenly Rusty had another idea.

"My grandmother's a painter," he said. "Will you buy one of her paintings?"

"No, I'm afraid not," said the man.

"Please?" said Rusty.

"What's your grandmother's name?" asked the man.

"Mary Morelli," said Rusty. "She lives on Baldwin Street. It's not very far from here."

The man smiled. "I can't say I know her name," he said. "But I tell you what. Leave your address. If I have a chance, I'll come by and take a look."

The man opened his jacket. He took a little card out of his inside pocket. He gave it to Rusty and said, "Please give this to your grandmother."

As they left the museum, Fizz Eddie and Rusty read the card. It said *William Snow*.

"Well, at least you finally saw snow," said Fizz Eddie. He was trying to make a joke to cheer Rusty up.

But Rusty couldn't laugh. He felt too sad. He had nothing to sell. And he had no money to bring his parents home.

Chapter 7

It was the day of the school party. The air was cold and the sun was shining.

"Cheer up, Champ," said Fizz Eddie. "I know you wish your parents were here. But your party will still be fun."

The first part of the party was a concert in the auditorium. Fizz Eddie and Kimberly were both in the junior high band. Fizz Eddie played the trumpet. Kimberly played the flute.

At one point Fizz Eddie stood up and played a solo.

"Bravo!" shouted someone from the back.

Rusty knew the voice. It was his grandmother. She was sitting with the parents in the back.

Rusty and his class sang their holiday medley. He was glad he remembered all the words.

"Bravo!" shouted his grandmother again.

"Bravo!" shouted another voice. It was Fizz Eddie! Rusty looked over at him. He was sitting with the junior high band. He gave the thumbs-up sign to Rusty.

Rusty smiled. He knew Fizz Eddie and his grandmother were trying extra hard to make him feel good.

After the concert, Mrs. Morelli went home. She didn't stay for the party. She said she had to go home and paint.

The party was okay. The Chinese food was good. Spinning the dreidel was fun. And the tree looked cool.

But then the hard part came. Kids gave their parents the Kwanzaa presents they had made.

Rusty gave his pencil holder to Mr. Carson.

"It holds twenty pencils," said Rusty.

"So it's mathematical," said Mr. Carson. "And I love it. Thank you very much, Rusty. This pencil holder is going to be one of my favorite presents this year."

Rusty could tell Mr. Carson was trying to make him feel good, too.

But it didn't work. Something about the party made his sadness feel worse.

When he got home, he saw his grandmother and a man on the porch.

It was Mr. Snow from the museum. He and Mrs. Morelli were putting up Christmas lights.

Rusty's grandmother gave Rusty a big hug. "Guess what?" she said. "Mr. Snow offered me two thousand dollars for my big painting!"

Rusty couldn't believe it. This was great news!

"But I told him that painting was yours and not for sale," said his grandmother.

"You what?" asked Rusty. "Hey, it's okay, Mr. Snow. You can buy it if you want."

"Wait a minute," said his grandmother. "I painted that painting just for you! So I showed Mr. Snow my other paintings. And he bought two of them for a thousand dollars each!"

"Yippee!" cried Rusty. "Now Mom and Dad can come home!"

"I've already called them. They'll be home Christmas Eve."

Rusty hugged his grandma, and Mr. Snow, too. He felt like all the dancing triangles in the big painting.

Then his grandma plugged in the Christmas lights. Suddenly the porch started blinking. Red, yellow, green, blue, and orange.

"I think there's a way to get them to stop blinking," said Mr. Snow.

"What for?" said Mrs. Morelli. "I want them to blink!"

Just then, Mary Kate's mother came by. She was carrying a box. The box was going, "Yip! Yip! Yip!"

Inside the box was an adorable brown puppy. "Yip! Yip!" he cried.

"Would you mind keeping this puppy for me until Christmas?" she asked. "I want him to be a surprise for Mary Kate."

"It's fine with me," said Mrs. Morelli. "Is it okay with you, Rusty?"

"Sure," said Rusty.

But inside, he was thinking about Mary Kate's ugly quilt. Should he tell Mary Kate to take it back and get a pretty one?

After Mr. Snow left, Rusty told his

grandmother about the ugly quilt.

Mrs. Morelli laughed.

"What should I do?" he asked.

"Don't worry about it," said his grandmother. "Orange flowers and purple leaves sound great to me. Maybe Mary Kate's mother will like it."

Chapter 8

On Christmas Eve day there was no school. Mary Kate called Rusty to see if he wanted to play.

"I can't," he said. "I'm making a picture for my mother. She's coming home this afternoon!"

"Can I come over and paint, too?" asked Mary Kate.

Rusty wanted to say yes. But he couldn't because of the puppy.

"Yip! Yip! Yip!" Rusty could hear the puppy in the kitchen.

"What's that noise?" asked Mary Kate.

"What noise?" said Rusty. "That must be Mr. O'Brien, working on the roof. You'd better not come over. He's making too much noise. I'll see you tomorrow."

"Okay," said Mary Kate. She sounded miserable.

Rusty wanted to tell her about the puppy. But he couldn't. He had promised not to.

He went back to his painting.

His grandmother was painting, too. Her painting was beginning to look like Christmas tree lights. "It's almost done," she said.

Rusty was making a painting of the Giving Tree. He thought his mother would like it because she liked helping poor people.

Rusty painted an eagle feather on top. Then he painted an eagle in the sky. Then a second one. And a third. And a fourth.

A whole family of eagles, including the grandmother, thought Rusty. He was so busy painting he lost track of time.

All of a sudden, there was noise on the porch. The door burst open. And in came Rusty's mom and dad!

They dropped their suitcases and held out their arms. Rusty and his grandmother ran into them.

Christmas Eve hadn't even come yet. But Rusty had already received his very best present. At last, he was happy, happy.

That night Rusty's mom called Michael's mom to find out about a church they could go to. Since Rusty's mom and dad didn't live in Appleville yet, they didn't belong to a church.

Michael's mom invited them to her church. It was a beautiful brick church a few blocks away. There were mostly black people in the church. And hundreds of red flowers.

Michael was up front in the children's choir. He was wearing a blue-and-gold robe. The choir sounded strong and good.

After they sang, they walked down the

aisle. Michael Finn saw Rusty and waved. "Want to be in the pageant?" he asked. "One of our shepherds is sick."

"Can I?" asked Rusty. He looked at his mom.

"Go ahead," she said.

"Come on," said Michael.

So Rusty walked out with the choir. A few minutes later he walked in as a shepherd.

He stood in the front of the church with a staff in his hand. His friend Alexandra was Mary. She was holding a baby doll in her arms. Michael Finn was Joseph.

The pastor of the church read a story about how Jesus was born in a manger. He said shepherds came with their sheep to see him. Rusty felt proud to be a shepherd. He imagined that the doll in Alexandra's arms really was Baby Jesus.

"Christmas is Jesus's birthday party," said the pastor.

Happy Birthday, Jesus, thought Rusty.

*   *   *

Rusty and his parents came home from church. In the middle of the living room was the finished painting. It had a big red bow and a tag on it.

To Rusty. Love, Grandma, read the tag.

Rusty hugged his grandmother and thanked her. "I'd like to put it in the hall," he said, "so Santa Claus won't think he's in a museum when he comes down the chimney."

Rusty's mom and dad moved the painting to the hall. "It can't stay in the hall for long," said his dad, "because you have to move it to go up and down the stairs."

"I'll put it somewhere else soon," said Rusty. He didn't know where. But he didn't want to worry about it on Christmas Eve. He had another worry on his mind.

"Is there really a Santa?" he asked his mother.

"Of course there is," she said.

Rusty sat beside her on the living room couch. It was nice to have the living room be normal again. And it was great to be with his mom.

Rusty looked at the chimney. "Does Santa know we moved to New Jersey?" he asked.

"Yes," said his mother. "I wrote and told him."

"My samurai sword won't fall on him, will it?" asked Rusty.

"No," said his mother.

"What if Santa doesn't like granola bars?" asked Rusty. He looked at the snack his grandmother had put out.

"He will," said his mother.

"Don't build a fire in the fireplace," said Rusty.

"We won't," said his mother. "And now I think it's time for you to go to bed. Santa won't come until you're asleep."

Chapter 9

Christmas afternoon, most of the kids on Baldwin Street went outside to play. Everyone had something new to show off.

Michael Finn had a bag full of army men and a Jets jacket.

"I thought you liked the Giants," said Rusty.

"I do," said Michael. "But my aunt got the teams mixed up. It's okay. I like the Jets, too. Maybe the Jets jacket will bring them good luck."

"Maybe it will help you grow your teeth," said Jane.

Jane had her hands tucked into a new rabbit-fur muff. "It's fake," she said happily. "But it feels just like real."

Mary Kate had her new puppy on a leash. "I named him Sugar because he's so sweet," she said.

"What about the quilt?" whispered Rusty.

Mary Kate's face turned red. "It was for me!" she said. "My father had *me* pick it out because it was his present for me!"

"What did you tell him?" asked Rusty.

Mary Kate rolled her eyes. "I said I loved it," she said. "Actually it's not that bad. I guess I wasn't *that* mad at my mother."

Rusty laughed.

"What did you get?" asked Mary Kate.

It was the question Rusty had been waiting for. "A drum from Brazil," he said. "It's almost as big as I am."

"That's neat," said Fizz Eddie. "Go get it, and I'll get my keyboard."

Rusty's dad helped him carry his drum out to the street.

Rusty and Fizz Eddie sat on Mary Kate's stoop. Fizz Eddie already knew how to play a lot of tunes. Rusty tapped his drum lightly to keep the beat.

They played "The Mexican Hat Dance," "The Dreidel Song," and "I'm Dreaming of a White Hanukkah."

As they played, little white stars began to fall from the sky.

"Is that snow?" asked Rusty.

"That's it, Champ," said Fizz Eddie. "How do you like it?"

"It's the most beautiful thing in the world," said Rusty.

Chapter 10

It was January 2nd. The holidays were over. Everyone was back in school.

"Let's go over the chart," said Michael. "To see if everyone got what they wanted. I'll go first. I got my army men but not my teeth."

"I got my puppy," said Mary Kate. Rusty noticed that she didn't say a word about the quilt.

"I got a fake rabbit-fur muff," said Jane.

"I got a racing car," said John. "And look what else I got."

John stood up proudly. He was wearing a new belt. It had a silver belt buckle shaped like an eagle. "The eagle flies highest of all the birds," said John.

"That's awesome," said Rusty.

"I got a Barbie doll and four Barbie outfits," said Maria.

"I got ice skates," said Lisa. "What about you, Rusty?"

Rusty's best present had gone back to the jungle. So he was feeling a little down. But he tried to cheer up. "I got a drum and snow," he said. "I was very lucky."

Everybody in the class had gotten what they wanted or something different and better.

"What about you?" John asked Mr. Carson.

Mr. Carson looked up at the big crack in the wall. "I guess Santa didn't come to the Appleville School," he said.

Suddenly Rusty had such a good idea that he felt like Santa Claus. After school he ran home and told his grandmother. She liked the idea, too. And she told Mr. O'Brien.

The next day when Rusty walked to school, he was accompanied by Mr. and Mrs. Santa Claus. They were carrying the biggest present anyone had ever seen.

Everyone in the schoolyard stared at them.

Mr. and Mrs. Claus carried the present through the green door. They carried it right into Mr. Carson's room.

"Merry Christmas," said Rusty. "It's really my grandmother and the roofer," he told everyone.

"And a Happy New Year, too," said Mrs. Claus.

"Ho, ho, ho!" said Santa. "Where do we put it?"

"Right up there over the crack," said Rusty. "But first Mr. Carson has to unwrap it."

Mr. Carson smiled and said, "I wonder if someone could give me a hand."

Immediately the kids in the room tore off the wrapping paper.

There stood the big painting. Mr. Carson was amazed and delighted. "This is the best present ever," he said.

There were already two hooks in the wall. And two stepladders in place.

"Who put them there?" asked John.

"Who do you think?" said Santa.

He and Mr. Carson carried the painting up the ladders and hung it on the wall. The painting covered the whole crack.

"It's a jungle," said Mary Kate.

"It's the Ice Capades," said Lisa.

"It's mathematical," said Mr. Carson. "It's like Michael's map of your block."

Everyone looked at Michael Finn's Christmas map, which was hanging nearby.

Mr. Carson picked up his pointer. He pointed at one of the triangles on the painting and started to count. "One, two, three. . ." Soon everyone joined in. They

went right on counting until they reached 37, 38, 39.

"It's a painting of the 39 kids on the block, right?" said Mr. Carson.

"Right," said Mrs. Claus. "Isn't it wonderful how everyone always knows what my paintings are about?"

About the Author

"I like writing about children and their families," says author Jean Marzollo. "Children are never boring. Whenever I get stuck for an idea, I visit a classroom and talk to the kids. They give me millions of ideas, and all I have to do is choose the right one.

"I remember everything about elementary school—my teachers' names, the lamp with painted roses on it that we gave the teacher when she got married, who cried on the playground and why, and how to make fish with finger paint.

"When I write the stories for *39 Kids on the Block*, I draw on my childhood memories and my experiences in schools today. I also live with my two teenage sons and my husband in Cold Spring, New York, a community with strong values and lots of stories."

About the Illustrator

"Jean Marzollo and I have been the best of friends for more than 20 years, and we have also worked together on many books," says illustrator Irene Trivas. "She writes about kids; I draw them.

"Once upon a time we both lived in New York and learned all about living in the city. Then we moved away. I went off to Vermont and had to learn how to live in the country. But the kids we met were the same everywhere: complicated, funny, silly, serious, and more imaginative than any grown-up can ever be."

Irene Trivas has illustrated a number of picture books and easy-to-read books for children. She has also written and illustrated her own book, *Emma's Christmas: An Old Song* (Orchard).

More fun with
39 Kids on the Block.
Look for #3!

Roses Are Pink and You Stink!

Roses are red,
Roses are pink.
Rusty Morelli,
You stink!

Michael Finn is angry with
everyone—Rusty and Mary Kate
and John and even Mr. Carson.
Now he'll get back at them all!

How many kids live on your block?

200 Winners!

Enter the

39 Kids on the Block™

Giveaway!
WIN A BACKPACK!

Wouldn't it be neat to carry all your favorite things in a fun backpack? You can win one! Enter the **"39 Kids on the Block" Giveaway.** Just tell us how many kids live near you on your block, in your neighborhood, or in your apartment building. Then fill in the coupon below, and return by March 31, 1990.

Rules: Entries must be postmarked by March 31, 1990. Winners will be picked at random and notified by mail. No purchase necessary. Valid only in the U.S.A. Void where prohibited. Taxes on prizes are the responsibility of the winners and their families. Employees of Scholastic Inc.; its agencies, affiliates, subsidiaries; and their immediate families not eligible. For a complete list of winners, send a stamped, self-addressed envelope to The 39 Kids on the Block Giveaway, Contest Winners List, at the address provided below.

Fill in the coupon below or write the information on a 3" x 5" piece of paper and mail to: **THE 39 KIDS ON THE BLOCK GIVEAWAY**, Scholastic Inc., P.O. Box 673, Cooper Station, New York, NY 10276.

- -

The *39 Kids on the Block* Giveaway

How many kids live on/in your block? _____ Neighborhood? _____

Apartment building? _____ Other? _____

Name _____ Age _____

Street _____

City _____ State _____ Zip _____

Where did you buy this *39 Kids on the Block* book?
- ❏ Bookstore ❏ Drug Store ❏ Supermarket
- ❏ Discount Store ❏ Book Club ❏ Book Fair ❏ Other_____(specify)

KOB489